Pete

THE CROW

Pete
THE CROW

André Dugo

THE VIKING PRESS · NEW YORK · 1949

To
Joan Margaret

THERE was a tall tree in the midst of the forest, and in its very highest branches was a big nest. It was built roughly of twigs and straw. It was ugly outside, but it was warm and cozy inside, padded with grass and feathers.

6

There lived Pete the little crow, with his sister and brother.
There were, of course, Papa Crow and Mamma Crow, too, who
came home every so often with a nice juicy worm or bug to
feed the children.

7

They taught them to speak and say nicely, "Caw-caw-caw," when they were hungry, which in crow-language means, "please." And because they were hungry all the time, they had their little yellow beaks open and said, "Caw-caw-caw," all day long.

Whenever Papa or Mamma Crow flew away for business, to hunt for insects or other food, they always warned the little birds:

"Now, be careful. Don't put your head out of the nest, and, especially, don't lean or climb over the edge because you might fall. We are here on the top floor, and, as you can't fly yet, you would break your little necks."

So when they were left alone the little crows could look up at the sky, look at the leaves and the branches, watch the grown-up birds fly by, and caw-caw with each other till their parents came home. But one day a bee lighted on the edge of the nest.

8

Pete wanted to show his brother and sister that he could catch
the bee all by himself. He stood up in the nest and took a step
toward the edge. Then he climbed up a little, stuck out his neck
quickly, and there! the bee flew away—but Pete was out of the

9

nest and falling down, down, down the tree.

10

He was lucky. A few branches slowed up his fall and he landed first on a big bush under the tree, then on a big clump of grass under the bush, so that he arrived on the ground with a few bruises but without breaking his bones.

Now there he was, all alone, rubbing his body with his beak where it hurt, and looking up desperately, but he couldn't even see the nest, it was so far up in the branches. He heard his mother and father arrive and call for him till late in the night, "Caw, caw," which means, "Pete, where are you?" He tried to answer, but his voice was too weak. They didn't hear him. It was dark, he was hungry and alone. He cried and cried, till he cried himself to sleep.

He woke up next morning hearing voices: "Look, Father, a little bird has fallen out of the nest," and two hands lifted him up gently from the ground.

"That's a little crow, Tom. If you promise to take good care of him, you can bring him home."

That's how Pete came to the farmer's house and was given a part of the chickencoop, which was cleaned up for him, to live in.

When he was asked what his name was, he was still so frightened that only little sounds came out of his throat, "peet, peet"—so he was called Pete, which really was his name.

He was well fed and grew up to be a handsome, shiny black young crow. The farmer put a bright metal band around one

12

of his legs. Pete learned to know his master, Tom, Tom's father and mother, and the hired man, and soon he forgot about the nest he was born in, and about the forest and his own family.

He wasn't kept in a cage, but flew freely around the house and the yard. He played with Tom, sat on his shoulder, ate from his hand. In the morning he said, "Hello," which sounded rather like "Caw-caw," and it was impossible to shoo him away from the breakfast table, where he shared with Tom the peanut-butter-jelly-bread. After breakfast he liked to fly out in the yard and play with the dog Freckles. He would steal a bone from Freckles' plate and wait a few yards away until the dog gave chase. Then he would fly away a little farther and wait till it started all over again. It was a good game.

He teased the hens, who were
afraid he would take away the little
chickens, and it was a great joke to make the old peaceful gray
horse jump in the air by landing
suddenly on his head.

He became such a tease that he couldn't leave anybody alone.
He frightened the little ducks by swooping down suddenly

16

from the air over their heads, and when they ran in a panic he
laughed, "Caw-caw."

With the cat, Buffy, he had learned to be more careful ever since the day when a few feathers from his tail had remained in Buffy's paw.

But except for the cat, he wasn't afraid of anybody. He didn't have respect even for Tom's father, the farmer. When the

18

farmer worked out in the garden, Pete sat on his shoulder or landed on top of his hat, and wouldn't go away until the farmer, laughing, scratched his head or his throat. Then Pete would close his eyes, rub his beak against the farmer's cheek, and be very happy.

Pete was a nice jolly fellow, a great tease, but he didn't mean any harm. He just wanted to play. Everyone liked him, especially Tom—and maybe that was his downfall. He thought he could do anything—everything was permitted.

The trouble started when one day a silver spoon was missing from the table. Next day another spoon went. The third day the farmer's wife just caught Pete when he was about to fly away with a third spoon.

20

"No, my friend," she said, "that can't go on," and to punish Pete she put him in a cage.

Little Tom cried and begged his mother, and Pete looked so forlorn that the next day she let him out again.

But Pete was spoiled now and hadn't yet learned his lesson. That's how he came to the disastrous afternoon which made the turning point in his life. As he couldn't get at home the new shiny things he liked so much, the first thing he did when he was free again was to fly over to the neighbors'.

Mrs. Shoemaker was having coffee with some friends on her porch when Pete zoomed down from the air to snatch the spoon which was on her saucer. Naturally, the whole cup of

coffee went into her lap, on her brand-new dress. In the excite-
ment Pete dropped the spoon, and the ladies were so frightened
that one of them fainted.

As he hadn't got the spoon, Pete tried to steal the nice silk hair-ribbon from Mrs. Shoemaker's little Barbara. That turned out very badly. His feet got so entangled in the ribbon and in the little girl's hair that her mother, hearing her shrieks, had to run out from the porch and free her from Pete. Pete said, "Caw-caw," meaning, "I am sorry, I didn't mean to hurt her," but the harm was done. The lady was very angry and gave him a good slap with the broom.

"I certainly am not popular with the Shoemakers today," thought Pete, and flew away toward the minister's house.

The minister's wife was out in her garden. You might think that by now Pete ought to have known better. But no! When he saw the gold clasp glittering on her bead necklace, he couldn't resist. He dropped down onto her back, and, heavens! in what a state she was when she finally got him away. Her blouse was torn, the beads were scattered all over the ground—and the old lady was very near to tears.

But Pete's worst joke came after that. He had failed with the spoon, the ribbon, and the necklace, so now he stole the eyeglasses right off the nose of the minister, who was having a nap in a deckchair on the lawn. Pete wanted to play the same game which he played with Freckles the dog. The poor old gentleman chased him, and, when he thought he was about to catch him, Pete moved just a few steps farther away. That went on for

half an hour, until the old man sat down exhausted—and Pete dropped the eyeglasses, which were, of course, broken.

So before the afternoon was over everybody in the neighborhood was boiling mad. They called Pete a pest and came to the farmer demanding that he do something about it.

"I will cut his wings," said the farmer, "so he can't fly to the neighbors' and annoy everyone."

Tom cried, Pete said, "Caw-caw," but it didn't help. His wing feathers were cut.

Pete was very sad. He couldn't fly any more; he could only hop around in the garden like a hen. His little master Tom had tears in his eyes whenever he saw Pete jumping awkwardly about.

"Poor Pete," he said. "I wish I had never brought you home, if you have to live like a prisoner."

One day when Pete was walking sadly in the yard, he heard "Caw-caw-caw," and there was another crow at the top of the chickencoop. It was just like Pete, only a little smaller and slimmer. It was a lady crow.

She said, "Caw-caw-caw," which means in crow language, "My name is Melinda. Who are you?"

Pete answered, "Caw-caw. How do you do? My name is Pete."

"Why do you stay here?" said Melinda. "Come with me to the woods, where the other crows live."

"If I only could," said Pete, "but I can't fly," and he showed her his cut wing feathers.

"That comes from staying with men," said she, "but don't worry. They will grow again and I will come back for you."

29

And after a while his feathers did grow again, and one evening Melinda came for him. First he had to try out his new wings. He flew to the top of the chickencoop, then from there to the big apple tree. Tom called his father excitedly.

"Father, Father, look! Pete can fly again—and there is another crow with him."

The farmer looked at the birds and said, smiling, "Yes, son, and it seems to me we will lose Pete. He has found a mate."

"You mean Pete will fly away and I won't have him any more?" asked Tom.

"I am afraid so, Tommy," the farmer said. "You see, wild birds, however tame they are, like their freedom."

Tommy had two big tears in his eyes, but he smiled bravely and said, "I am glad for him. I'd rather he'd fly away than have his wing feathers cut again. But maybe he will come back to see us sometime."

"Maybe," said the farmer. "Maybe."

At that moment Pete and Melinda rose from the tree and made a few circles in the air over the house. Pete said, "Caw-caw" to Tom, which meant, "Good-by." Tom waved his hand and yelled, "Good luck!" Then the birds flew away to the woods.

30

When Pete was presented to the other crows they turned their beaks in the air and said, "Caw-caw-caw-caw," meaning, "He smells strange. He smells like a man-child. He is not a crow."

"Yes, he is," said Melinda, "only he lived so long with people. That's why he smells like a man-child."

The oldest crow said, "Then he'd better take a bath before he comes to live with us." So Pete went to the nearest brook and washed himself from head to foot, and came back shiny and black and smelling as a young crow should smell.

31

Later he and Melinda built a rough nest of twigs and straw, on the top of the tallest tree in the forest, and very soon there were three little crows in the nest—their children.

And every time he has to fly away to catch worms and bugs for the little crows, Pete says very seriously: "Caw-caw. Now be careful. Don't put your heads out of the nest, and, especially, don't lean or climb over the edge, because you might fall."